Bee Attitudes
Bee Peaceful

by Ron & Carrie Webb
illustrated by Sal Garcia

"There is peace with God through Jesus Christ."
Acts 10:36

Author's Note to Parents:

When I was in 6th grade, I thought I had committed the unpardonable sin that I heard about in Sunday School. 😠 I struggled with fear, condemnation and guilt to the point that I had trouble falling asleep at night. So I prayed to receive Jesus as my Savior every Sunday, yet I still did not experience God's peace. After a year of torment, the fear left when I resolved to serve God whether I was going to hell or not. I wish I had understood the truth as a child that Jesus took our punishment for sin so that we could be made righteous in Christ and enjoy His peace! "There is peace with God through Jesus Christ!" Acts 10:36.

Up in a tree,
hanging down from above,
a beehive busily buzzing God's love.

Papa Bee, Mama Bee, Chubbee and Bree
buzzing God's love.
Take a look and you'll see.

Chubbee buzzed home,
his wings were all droopy.
Chubbee felt bad
and his eyes were soupy!

Soupy from crying,
his tears in a puddle.
He hid in his room,
his head in a muddle.

At supper time, Mama, Papa and Bree
buzzed around wondering,
"Where could he be?"

They looked in the honey pot,
looked in his bed.
They looked 'round the tree
and scratched their bee heads!

"Where is that Chubbee?" they quietly thought.
Then Papa heard something that made the thought
STOP!

It was like a sob from a heart broken.
"Chubbee?" they called...
but nothing was spoken.

They buzzed to his room for another good look.
They found Chubbee crying...
UNDER A BOOK!

"Chubbee!" called Mama,
"Please tell me what's wrong!
Why are you crying?
Have you been here long?"

"Mama!" sobbed Chubbee,
"I did something bad!
I can't stop crying
and feeling so sad!"

"While on my way home, I pulled a zinger!
A little kid got poked with my stinger!"

"I wasn't watching.
It was an accident.
The kid's really hurt!
And my stinger is bent!"

"Accidents happen,"
Papa said with a smile.
"A stinger that bent,
I've not seen in a while!"

"Papa!" scolded Mama, "You're no help at all!
Why don't you and Bree just buzz down the hall!"

"You're missing the point
if you think it's funny.
Chubbee's been crying,
his bee nose is runny!"

So after they left,
Mama looked at her bee.
"Why were you crying and hiding from me?"

Not knowing what's wrong, how can I help you?
Together we'll figure out what we can do."

Chubbee spoke softly,
"Mama, I'm a good bee
But I'm worried that
God might be mad at me!"

"I should have been paying attention. Instead,
I stung that boy...
stung him right in the head!"

"I left him there crying,
not sure what to do.
I should have prayed for him, Mama, like you!"

"Chubbee," said Mama,
"God is not mad!
It's true even when we've been acting bad!"

"God doesn't like it whenever we sin!
But He always loves us,
again and again!"

"Jesus was punished for your sins and mine!
Because of Him,
God loves us all of the time!"

"Now there is peace between
God and men.
That peace comes to us
when we're born again!"

Chubbee asked, "Is it true?
God's not mad at me?"
"Never!" said Mama, most confidently!

"What about when we don't do things God's way?"
"Even then," Mama answered,
"God doesn't sway!"

"But it's never too late
to do the right thing."
Mama smiled at Chubbee,
"You know what I mean?"

Without even thinking,
Chubbee started to pray.
"Little boy, be healed
And pain go away!

In Jesus' name!"
Chubbee added, "Amen.
I'm thankful for God's peace
and goodwill to men!"

Jesus, I believe You are the Son of God.
You died on the cross as punishment for my sin.
You rose from the dead and
You are alive today.
Jesus, I receive You as my Lord and Savior.
Thank You for forgiving all my sins
and making me Your child.
In Jesus' name, Amen.

"If you openly declare that Jesus is Lord and believe in your heart that God raised Him from the dead, you will be saved. For it is by believing in your heart that you are made right with God, and it is by openly declaring your faith that you are saved... For everyone who calls on the name of the Lord will be saved."

Romans 10:9-10,13

About the Authors

Having a foundational belief that children can be valid members of God's family today, Ron and Carrie Webb develop creative, entertaining and inspirational materials that kids can understand, enjoy and apply.

The Webbs have been happily married since 1979. They are the parents of six children and nine grandchildren. They served together in full-time ministry at Abundant Living Faith Center in El Paso, TX, for 33½ years as Children's Pastors from 1984-2017, Youth Pastors from 1985-2000 and Performing Arts Ministry Directors from 2000-2017.

Special Thanks

Sal Garcia for illustrations
(ghostillustrator@gmail.com)

Ray Sanchez for editing
(ray@ghostlightcreative.com)

MORE FOR YOU

Made in the USA
Middletown, DE
25 September 2020